Airy Fairy

Magic Mix-Up!

D1584634

2213841

Look out for more stories...

Magic Mischief!

Magic Muddle!

Magic Mess!

Airy Fairy
Magic Mix-Up!

Margaret Ryan

illustrated by Teresa Murfin

SCHOLASTIC

To Millie with love

Scholastic Children's Books,
Euston House, 24 Eversholt Street,
London NW1 1DB, UK
a division of Scholastic Ltd
London ~ New York ~ Toronto ~ Sydney ~ Auckland
Mexico City ~ New Delhi ~ Hong Kong

First published by Scholastic Ltd, 2005

Text copyright © Margaret Ryan, 2005
Illustrations copyright © Teresa Murfin, 2005

10 digit ISBN 0 439 96335 4
13 digit ISBN 978 0439 96335 0

Printed and bound by Nørhaven Paperback A/S, Denmark

6 8 10 9 7 5

Chapter One

It was the last day of the summer term at Fairy Gropplethorpe's Academy for Good Fairies and the fairies were busy tidying out their desks.

"Be sure to clear out all the rubbish," said their teacher, Miss Stickler, "and put it in the bin."

Airy Fairy stopped gazing out of the classroom window at the swallows flitting by, lifted up the lid of her desk, and stuck her head inside. "My desk's not really full of rubbish," she said to her friends, Buttercup and Tingle. "It's just full of things that might be really useful one day. Like this empty yoghurt pot. I could keep all my pens and pencils in it." And she carefully tidied them into it and sat it on top of her desk. Then she opened her desk lid again, knocked over the yoghurt pot, and scattered the pens and pencils on to the floor.

"Oops," she said, and bent to pick them up.
Scary Fairy, whose desk was always tidy,
smiled slyly and waved her little wand.
Suddenly the pens and pencils started rolling
all over the floor. Airy Fairy crawled round
after them, but, as soon as she reached out
for them, they rolled even further away.

"Airy Fairy, what ARE you doing?"
frowned Miss Stickler,
when she saw Airy
Fairy's bottom
sticking in
the air.

"Sorry, Miss Stickler," gasped Airy Fairy, standing up and banging her head on Scary Fairy's desk. "I was trying to pick up my pens and pencils. They keep rolling away from me."

"Nonsense," said Miss Stickler, looking at the now perfectly still pens and pencils. "Pick them up at once and get on with your tidying."

"Yes, Miss Stickler," sighed Airy Fairy.

Scary Fairy gave Airy Fairy a sly poke with her wand. "Stupid fairy," she smirked.

Airy Fairy poked her right back.

"And stop poking Scary Fairy with your wand, or you'll have extra school work to do, even if it IS the last day of term," warned Miss Stickler.

"Yes, Miss Stickler," sighed Airy Fairy again. It was always the same. Scary Fairy, who was Miss Stickler's niece, always picked on her. Airy Fairy didn't know why.

"Never mind, Airy Fairy," whispered Buttercup and Tingle, when Airy Fairy had picked up her pens and pencils and sat down again. "We'll give you a hand to clear out your desk."

In no time at all, they helped Airy Fairy throw out all the broken pencils, all the scrunched-up paper, and all the half-chewed toffees. Not forgetting the empty yoghurt pot.

"There," they beamed. "Now you're ready for the summer holidays."

"Thank you," said Airy Fairy, and cupped her chin in her hands and smiled. She really 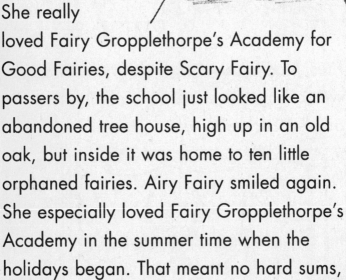 loved Fairy Gropplethorpe's Academy for Good Fairies, despite Scary Fairy. To passers by, the school just looked like an abandoned tree house, high up in an old oak, but inside it was home to ten little orphaned fairies. Airy Fairy smiled again. She especially loved Fairy Gropplethorpe's Academy in the summer time when the holidays began. That meant no hard sums, no difficult spelling, and no tricky flying-backwards lessons. She had enough trouble flying forwards. Now it was six long weeks of doing nothing but play.

"Hooray for the holidays," she cried, as the classroom door opened and Fairy Gropplethorpe came in, accompanied by Rainbow and MacDuff.

"I'm glad to see you all looking so happy, Fairies," smiled Fairy Gropplethorpe. "And since you have worked so hard this term, I have a surprise for you. You are all going on a special holiday. There will be no hard sums and no difficult spelling to do, so you can leave your fairy wands behind."

"Ooh, are we going to the seaside again?" asked Airy Fairy. "I just love the seaside. I love splashing about in the rock pools. I love making sandcastles. Can we have a sandcastle competition like we did last year? I'm going to try to make one with turrets and a moat and..."

"Airy Fairy, do be quiet and listen to Fairy Gropplethorpe."

"Yes, Miss Stickler. Sorry, Miss Stickler. Sorry, Fairy Gropplethorpe."

Fairy Gropplethorpe smiled again. "I know you're all excited about the holidays, but I'm afraid I won't be able to take you to the seaside this year. I have just discovered some dry rot in the school roof and must stay here till the builders arrive to fix it. But Miss Stickler has kindly volunteered to take you all on holiday, though I don't think it's to the seaside."

"Oh." Airy Fairy's face fell.

"No," said Miss Stickler. "This year we're not going to the seaside to get ourselves covered in gritty brown sand. This year we're going to do something much more educational. This year we're going camping."

"Camping?" Airy Fairy's face fell even further. "Oh, I don't think I'll like that. There are bound to be creepy crawly things, and busy buzzy things, and big ENORMOUS spiders…"

"I've had a letter," went on Miss Stickler, "from my friend Miss Snippersnap, of Fairy Topnob's School for Superior Fairies, and she has invited us to share a campsite with her and her pupils. We'll be sleeping in tents and cooking outdoors. Won't that be interesting? Miss Snippersnap's fairies are very clever girls, so I know you'll all do your best to be well behaved and not let your school down." And she looked meaningfully at Airy Fairy.

Airy Fairy didn't notice. She was too busy worrying about the camping and the spiders. There was a lot that could go wrong for a fairy in a field.

"It sounds splendid," said Fairy Gropplethorpe, "and I shall join you as soon as I can. Meanwhile, off you go and have fun."

And Fairy Gropplethorpe bustled away with Rainbow and MacDuff to worry about the school roof.

"Now, Fairies," said Miss Stickler. "Here is a list of what you need to take for the camping holiday, so hurry along to your bedrooms and pack your rucksacks. We're leaving this afternoon."

"Oh dear," said Airy Fairy, picking up her copy of the list. "I don't think I want to sleep on a door or cook a tent. I'm sure to get it all wrong. I'm sure this holiday will be a disaster."

"No, it won't," soothed Buttercup and Tingle. "Stop worrying, Airy Fairy. You'll be fine."

"No, you won't," muttered Scary Fairy slyly. "I'm sneaking my wand with me, and I'll see that you're not."

Chapter Two

Airy Fairy flew upstairs to her bedroom to look for her little rucksack.

"I think that might be one of its red straps hanging down from my big cupboard," she said, and gave the strap a tug. WHUMPH. Down came the rucksack on top of her, along with a bucket and spade, a pair of flippers and some goggles, and some pink and white stripy sunglasses.

"Oh," she gasped, picking herself up from the floor. "I wondered where all those things had gone." And she looked at the list Miss Stickler had given her. "But I'm not supposed to pack any of them for this holiday." Instead she had to pack her anorak and wellies, her bobble hat and scarf, and a big warm jumper.

"Those don't sound very much like holiday things," said Airy Fairy. "Perhaps Miss Stickler's forgotten to mention a swimsuit and

some shorts. I'd better put mine in anyway.
And my flippers and goggles. You can't go
swimming without flippers and goggles. And
what about my snorkel? I'd better put that in
as well."

Then she sat back and looked at the list again.
"It doesn't say anything about jigsaws either,"
she muttered. "I always like to do a jigsaw on
holiday." And she rummaged in the bottom of
her cupboard, found one of her favourites and
popped that in her rucksack too.

"Oh, and I mustn't forget pocket Ted. He likes to go on holiday as well." And she tied a scarf round Ted's neck and put him in the pocket of her pink fairy jeans. She left his head sticking out.

"So you can see where we're going, Ted," she explained.

Then she tried to fasten her rucksack. It wasn't easy. It was full of lumps and bumps. She had to jump on them to squash them down.

Airy Fairy's face was as pink as her jeans by the time she'd got the rucksack fastened. Then she looked round at the bucket and spade and pink and white stripy sunglasses still lying on her bedroom floor.

"I might need these too," she said. And she found a bit of string and tied the bucket and spade on to the outside of the rucksack, and put on her sunglasses.

"Right, Ted. Here we go."

But they didn't. Airy Fairy puffed and panted, and panted and puffed, but she couldn't even lift the rucksack, never mind put it on her back.

"Oh dear," she said. "This is far too heavy for me. I'm going to have to try a spell to get it down into the hall."

Ted closed his eyes and crossed his paws.

Airy Fairy took off her sunglasses, found her wand and gave it a wave.

"ALL FOR ONE
AND ONE FOR ALL
PLEASE TAKE THIS RUCKSACK
TO THE HALL!"

WHOOSH, the rucksack sailed out through the bedroom door, down the stairs, straight into Miss Stickler, knocking her over.

"Oh help. Oh sorry, Miss Stickler," said Airy Fairy, dropping her wand and flying downstairs to help her. "I had just finished packing, but the rucksack was very heavy and I couldn't lift it, and I did a spell, but I don't think it could have been the right one, and I must have got it mixed up and..."

Airy Fairy patted Miss Stickler's head. "Is your head very sore? Can I get you a sticking plaster? Do you put sticking plasters on bumps? Or I could get you a wet flannel, or I could…"

"You will do nothing, Airy Fairy," cried Miss Stickler, staggering to her feet. "Nothing at all, except stand right here. Do not move from this spot. We haven't even left to go on holiday yet, and already you're in trouble. I hope you are not going to let the Academy down when we meet up with Miss Snippersnap's fairies."

"Yes, Miss Stickler. I mean no, Miss Stickler. I mean sorry, Miss Stickler. I just don't know what happened to that spell. I was sure I had got it right..."

"You had, till I mixed it up," giggled Scary Fairy to herself as she flew downstairs with her little rucksack. "And there are plenty more mix-ups where that came from, Airy Fairy. I don't know why everyone likes you so much. You're such an idiot. You're going to be an absolute disaster on this holiday. I've packed my wand to make sure of that."

Chapter Three

Miss Stickler had organized a toy Fairy
Tour bus to take the fairies to the campsite,
and, when it alighted at the foot of the
oak tree, all the fairies flew down and
put their rucksacks into the boot. All except
Airy Fairy.

"Your rucksack is far too heavy, Airy Fairy," frowned Miss Stickler. "But there is no time to unpack it now, or we will be late arriving at the campsite." And she waved her wand and magicked Airy Fairy's rucksack out of the school and down to the bus below.

Airy Fairy flew down after it. But she still couldn't lift it into the boot.

"Here, I'll give you a hand, little Fairy," said Elvis Elf, the bus driver. "Watcha got in here, anyway? The kitchen sink?" he puffed as he heaved it into the boot.

27

"Oh no, that wasn't on the list," said Airy Fairy, shaking her head.

Elvis Elf chuckled and went over to speak to Miss Stickler, so he didn't see Airy Fairy climb in after her rucksack to make sure her bucket and spade were still securely tied on.

She'd just finished checking when ... WHAM, the boot lid shut and Airy Fairy was left in the dark.

"Oh no," she cried. "Help! Help!" But no one could hear her above the noise of the bus starting up. "Help," she yelled again as she felt the bus judder along the ground and start to lift off into the air. "Help," she yelled again as the front of the bus tilted upwards and she slid and banged her head on the inside of the boot.

And, she might have spent the whole journey to the campsite in the boot of the bus, if Buttercup and Tingle hadn't noticed she was missing and alerted Miss Stickler.

Suddenly Airy Fairy felt her ears go pop as the bus descended quickly, juddered along the ground again and came to a halt back at the foot of the oak tree. She yelled and thumped her spade on the inside of the boot.

"That can only be Airy Fairy," sighed Miss Stickler.

Elvis Elf and Miss Stickler got out of the bus and opened up the boot. They found Airy Fairy still yelling, "Help, get me out of here," and banging on the side of the bus with her spade.

"AIRY FAIRY," it was Miss Stickler's turn to yell. "Get on to the bus this minute and DO not move a muscle till we get to the campsite. In fact, DO nothing. SAY nothing. DO you understand?"

Airy Fairy looked at her with big eyes and said nothing.

"DO YOU UNDERSTAND?" Miss Stickler yelled even louder.

Airy Fairy looked at her with even bigger eyes and still said nothing.

"CAN YOU HEAR ME?" yelled Miss Stickler.

"I should think half the country can hear you," muttered Elvis Elf. "Glad I'm not still at school."

This time Airy Fairy nodded her head slightly and hurried on to the bus. *I wish teachers wouldn't tell you to say nothing then ask you questions,* she thought. *It makes life very difficult.*

The Fairy Tour bus took off again, and, after passing over lots of patchwork fields and little villages, alighted at the campsite. It was in a muddy field with enormous cows.

"Ah, Miss Stickler," said Miss Snippersnap, hurrying forwards to meet them. "You and your fairies are here at last. I was beginning to think you'd got lost. That's your accomodation over there." And she pointed to a row of tents.

"Oh no," said Airy Fairy, who had decided it was safe to speak by now. "I hope these cows don't notice our tents. I hope they don't think I'm lunch."

"Of course they won't," said Buttercup and Tingle. "Cows only eat grass, and anyway we're so small they won't even see us."

"That's what you think," muttered Scary Fairy. "I'm sure I can have some fun with them."

Miss Stickler showed the fairies to their tents. "Now, unpack your things, and assemble at my tent in fifteen minutes when you hear me peep my silver whistle," she said.

Airy Fairy's tent was right beside Miss Stickler's. "I've put you where I can keep an eye on you, Airy Fairy," she said. "I don't want you causing any more trouble."

"Yes, Miss Stickler. I mean no, Miss Stickler," muttered Airy Fairy, and ducked into her tent.

It was tiny inside. Hardly enough room for
Airy Fairy, never mind her bulging rucksack.
"What's this?" she said, spotting a rolled-up
bundle at the far end. "It must be my
sleeping bag. I've never slept in one of those
before. I'd better unroll it and try it out while
it's still daytime. It might be a bit tricky
tonight by torchlight."

Airy Fairy unrolled the sleeping bag,
climbed inside and zipped herself up.

"Hmm," she said, rolling round on the ground, trying to get comfortable. "I think I'd rather have my little fairy bed at school." And she rolled about a bit more, and knocked over her rucksack. It knocked over the tent pole and the tent fell down on top of her.

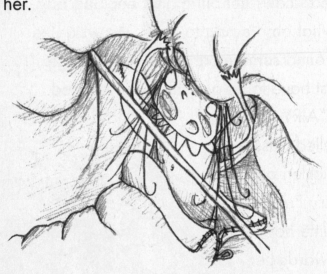

"Oh help," muttered Airy Fairy. "It's gone all dark. I must fix this tent before Miss Stickler notices. I'm in enough trouble already." And she propped the tent pole back up as best she could. "Now, I'll just get myself out of this sleeping bag."

But she couldn't. The zip had caught in her fairy jeans, and, try as she might, she couldn't set herself free. She wriggled around for ages, then ... PEEP PEEP...

"Oh no," she cried. "That's Miss Stickler's whistle. I have to assemble outside her tent, and I can't get out of this sleeping bag. What am I going to do?" She wriggled around some more, but it was no use. "I'll just have to go like this," she gasped.

"AIRY FAIRY," yelled Miss Stickler, as Airy Fairy came hopping towards her wearing her sleeping bag.

"I'm sorry, Miss Stickler," panted Airy Fairy. "I was just trying out my sleeping bag before it got dark, and the zip stuck. The tent fell down on top of me too."

The other fairies started giggling. They just loved Airy Fairy. She always made them laugh. They all went to help her out of the sleeping bag.

All except Scary Fairy. She wasn't laughing and she didn't go to help. "I just don't understand it. Why does everyone like her so much?" she muttered. "She always gets things wrong."

Miss Stickler wasn't laughing either. Miss Snippersnap had noticed the commotion and had come to investigate.

"Not a very good start to your camping holiday, Miss Stickler," she sniffed. "None of MY fairies would be silly enough to get stuck in a sleeping bag."

Miss Stickler's face was grim as Miss Snippersnap strode off. The last thing she wanted was for her fairies to look bad. "Now Airy Fairy really is in trouble," she muttered.

Scary Fairy was delighted and patted the fairy wand in her pocket. *And I'm sure I can get her into lots more,* she thought.

Chapter Four

But Airy Fairy was determined to try to stay out of trouble, so, when Miss Stickler read out their camp duties, she listened very carefully.

"Silvie and Skelf are in charge of collecting water from the farm over yonder," said Miss Stickler, pointing to a long, grey structure, which to humans just looked like an upturned sink.

"Buttercup and Tingle and Cherri and Honeysuckle will go with them and carefully collect an egg for our tea. Twink and Plink will go and organize games with Miss Snippersnap and her fairies. Scary Fairy, since she is the most responsible fairy –" Miss Stickler stopped reading from her list, and beamed at her niece – "will be in charge of our campfire. And Airy Fairy, since she is the most irresponsible fairy, will collect the wood from the forest."

And Miss Stickler turned and frowned at Airy Fairy. "Even you should be able to do that without getting into trouble," she said.

Airy Fairy nodded and looked over at the forest. It was on the edge of the field behind their tents.

"I'll go right away," she said, anxious to please, and flew off. In two minutes she was there. "This forest is really nice," she said, as she flitted through the trees. "I wonder if I'll see any red squirrels." And she looked up through the branches. Then she remembered she was supposed to be looking for firewood and looked down at the ground. BOINK. She crashed into a large pine tree and slid down the trunk.

"Oh dear," she sighed, rubbing her bumps and bruises. "Nothing out of ten for looking where you're going, Airy Fairy," and she got up, straightened her wings, and began to look for firewood. There was plenty of dry kindling littering the forest floor and she soon had a large bundle.

"Miss Stickler is bound to be pleased with this," she said, beaming, and started to fly out of the forest. But she had gathered so much kindling that bits kept falling to the ground.

"Perhaps I'd better just walk back," she muttered, "or I'll have no wood left."

But there was a problem. The cows had moved and were in between her and the campsite.

Airy Fairy gulped and walked towards them. "Nice cows, good cows, never mind about a fairy and her wood, cows," she whispered.

"Mooooo," went the cows loudly.

Airy Fairy nearly jumped out of her boots and dropped all her wood.

She quickly picked it up again, keeping an anxious eye on the cows. "I'll just try and go round the edge of them," she muttered.

As quietly as she could, she tiptoed round the outside of the herd muttering to herself, "Cows are good, cows are nice, cows won't look at a fairy twice."

But Scary Fairy, waiting impatiently for the wood to arrive for the campfire, had spotted Airy Fairy tiptoeing away from the cows.

"Aha." She smiled slyly. "Now for a bit of fun." And, when no one was looking, she took out her wand and gave it a little wave.

Suddenly the cows lifted their heads and started to chase Airy Fairy.

"Help," cried Airy Fairy and flapped her battered wings and began to fly. Bit by bit, the wood for the campfire slipped from her grasp, and fell and bopped the cows on the nose.

This annoyed them even more and they chased Airy Fairy right back to the campsite, trampling all the tents as they passed.

Then they stopped as suddenly as they'd begun, looked a bit puzzled, and wandered back the way they had come.

"Now how on earth did that happen?" Airy Fairy wondered as she bumped down to the ground, exhausted.

Miss Stickler was almost speechless. "Airy Fairy, how could..."

"I couldn't help it, Miss Stickler," gasped Airy Fairy. "I had the firewood, and I was tiptoeing round the cows, but they started chasing me, and I lost it all." And she looked round at all the trampled tents. "Oh dear," she said. "Sorry, Miss Stickler."

"Sorry isn't good enough, Airy Fairy." Miss Stickler had recovered her power of speech. "Of course you could help it. Cows don't just start chasing fairies. As usual, this is all your fault."

Airy Fairy traced a circle on the grass with the toe of her boot. "Sorry, Miss Stickler."

But Miss Stickler wasn't finished yet. "Now Twink and Plink have arranged a game of rounders with Miss Snippersnap's fairies, but you will stay here and put up all the tents instead. Then you will go back and collect the wood you dropped WITHOUT disturbing the cows. Do you understand?"

"Yes, Miss Stickler," said Airy Fairy miserably. She would have liked to play a game of rounders. That sounded like fun.

Scary Fairy grinned victoriously.

Buttercup and Tingle offered to stay behind to help Airy Fairy with the tents, but Miss Stickler would not hear of it.

"Airy Fairy must learn to stay out of trouble," she said. And everyone went off leaving Airy Fairy alone.

Airy Fairy gave the biggest sigh in the universe and started sorting out the tents. Hammering in lots of tent pegs is hard work for one little fairy. When she had finished, she very cautiously flew back into the forest to collect the firewood. This time the cows didn't even look at her. They just went on contentedly eating the grass.

"Hmm, I wonder if Scary Fairy was up to her tricks that last time," said Airy Fairy. But by now, she was too tired to care.

Buttercup and Tingle looked into her tent when they came back from their game of rounders. "Come and sit round the campfire while we boil the egg for tea," they started to say. But Airy Fairy and pocket Ted were already tucked up in their little sleeping bag fast asleep.

Chapter Five

Next morning all the fairies were up bright and early, especially Airy Fairy.

"I'm starving," she said to Buttercup and Tingle. "I missed my bit of the boiled egg for tea last night."

Miss Stickler, wearing shorts and a woolly jumper, was making porridge in a big black pot over the campfire.

"Breakfast will be ready soon, Fairies," she said, beaming. "Just pop down to the stream to wash your hands and faces."

The fairies collected their sponge bags and towels and headed for the stream that bordered the field. When they arrived, Miss Snippersnap's fairies were already there.

"Where's the fairy who stampeded the cows?" they asked.

"Here she is," said Scary Fairy, pushing Airy Fairy to the front. "But look out for her, she's an idiot."

"She must be," laughed Miss Snippersnap's fairies. "No one from Fairy Topnob's school for Superior Fairies would ever do anything so stupid." And they all turned and ignored Airy Fairy. They lined up neatly at the edge of the stream, and dipped their face flannels delicately into the water.

Airy Fairy sighed and looked in her sponge bag. She had forgotten her face flannel.

Oh well, she thought. *I'll just have to flip water on my face instead.* And she bent down towards the stream. That's when she noticed the fish darting in and out among the pebbles on the stream bed.

"Oh," she breathed, "aren't they lovely. Just like flashing silver." And she leaned forward to get a closer look.

Scary Fairy saw her chance. When no one was watching she waved her little wand. Suddenly there was a huge gust of wind that WHOOSHED Airy Fairy sideways.

"Help!" gasped Airy Fairy, her legs and arms going everywhere.

"Help," gasped the Superior Fairies, as Airy Fairy banged into them and knocked them all over like a row of dominoes, and they toppled into the water.

"Ooh, aah, help!" they gasped, as they struggled, dripping, from the stream.

"You did that on purpose, you stupid, idiotic fairy." They rounded on Airy Fairy. "Just wait till Miss Snippersnap hears about this."

"Oh no," gasped Airy Fairy. "I didn't ... I don't know ... I mean ... what will Miss Stickler say now!"

Miss Stickler said plenty. She had been happily stirring her porridge when Miss Snippersnap arrived to tell her all about it. At great length.

"Just keep that silly fairy away from my girls," Miss Snippersnap warned Miss Stickler. "She is obviously a menace. I would never have invited you here if I'd known there would be so much trouble."

Miss Stickler wasn't pleased, and she certainly didn't believe Airy Fairy's story about a big wind coming and whooshing her sideways. "But the big wind didn't blow over anyone else, did it, Airy Fairy?" she stormed. "Just you, funnily enough."

"But Airy Fairy didn't mean it, Miss Stickler." Buttercup and Tingle tried to stand up for her. "It all just sort of happened. Like perhaps someone had brought their wand..."

Airy Fairy nodded. She had a good idea who that someone might be, but it wasn't nice to tell tales, and anyway Miss Stickler would never believe her.

But Miss Stickler wasn't listening. "I'm going to take the other fairies to collect milk from the farm, but you will remain here, Airy Fairy.

Scary Fairy will set the breakfast table and keep an eye on you. Take this wooden spoon and stir the porridge. Even you should be able to do that without getting into any more trouble."

"Yes, Miss Stickler," sighed Airy Fairy, and she took the wooden spoon. She looked into the big black pot. The porridge was making soft little plopping noises. Airy Fairy stirred the porridge gently and it heaved its way slowly round the pot.

"I don't really like being left alone with Scary Fairy when she's up to her tricks. She might magic up enormous spiders," she said, and looked round anxiously. "And I don't know if I really like porridge, but I'm so hungry I could eat three whole bowlsful." And she gave the porridge another gentle stir.

When the others were out of sight, and Airy Fairy was busy stirring, Scary Fairy peered out of her tent and saw another chance to get Airy Fairy into trouble. She smiled slyly and waved her little magic wand.

WHEEE. The porridge speeded up and started whizzing round in the pot.

"Help, what's happening?" cried Airy Fairy, trying to keep up with the porridge with her wooden spoon. "Stop, porridge. Stop!"

But the porridge didn't stop. Instead it whizzed round faster and faster and started making angry slurping noises.

"Stop, porridge. Stop!" yelled Airy Fairy. But the porridge began erupting like a little volcano, throwing splashes of porridge out of the pot and on to the grass.

"Stop, porridge. Stop!" yelled Airy Fairy, her little arm whizzing round, and nearly dropping off with the effort of trying to control the porridge.

But the porridge wouldn't stop. It threw out more and more splashes till the porridge pot was completely empty. The gloopy porridge was all over the ground, all over the campfire, which it had put out, and all over Airy Fairy.

Miss Stickler arrived back with the other fairies just in time to see Airy Fairy trying to scoop some of the grassy porridge back into the pot.

"I'm so sorry, Aunt Stickler," Scary Fairy said at once. "I don't know how she managed it. I just turned my back for a moment to go into the store tent to collect the bowls and spoons for the porridge, and look what happens."

"Don't worry, Scary Fairy," said Miss Stickler. "It's not your fault. It's not your fault that we shall have nothing but cold milk and dry biscuits for breakfast, instead of beautiful creamy porridge. As usual, this is all your fault, Airy Fairy. You will take that porridge pot down to the stream and give it a good clean."

Buttercup and Tingle offered to go and help Airy Fairy, but Miss Stickler wouldn't let them.

"Airy Fairy must be punished for her terrible behaviour. She never wanted to come on this holiday, and she's just trying to ruin it for everyone else. I will not have that."

And Airy Fairy had to lug the big porridge pot down to the stream and give it a good clean.

But, as soon as they could, Buttercup and Tingle slipped away and helped Airy Fairy bring the clean porridge pot back.

"Look," they whispered. "We kept you some biscuits. You must be starving."

"I am," said Airy Fairy, and had a quick nibble. "But I'm not trying to spoil the holiday for everyone else. Really I'm not."

"We know that," said Buttercup and Tingle. "It'll be Scary Fairy up to her dirty tricks again. But we'll help you keep an eye on her, and so will the other fairies."

"Thank you. But Scary Fairy's just too clever to get caught," sighed Airy Fairy. "This is such a rotten holiday, I almost wish I was back in school doing hard sums and difficult spelling. Surely things can't get any worse."

But they did.

Chapter Six

Later that day, it started to rain. Not a light, refreshing rain, but a heavy downpour that went on and on. Airy Fairy sat in her little tent with Ted. He was warm and dry in her pocket, but she was cold and wet as water dripped from the roof of her tent down the neck of her anorak, and seeped up from the ground through a hole in the sole of her welly.

But Miss Stickler didn't mind the rain. PEEP PEEP went her silver whistle.

"Come along, Fairies," she cried, "a little rain never hurt anyone. Miss Snippersnap's fairies are here to join us on a nature hunt."

"I'd like to hunt out somewhere dry," muttered Airy Fairy, as she squelched out of her tent and into a big puddle. Her right welly filled up with water and she had to take it off and empty it out.

"Hurry along, Airy Fairy," said Miss Stickler.

Airy Fairy tried to hurry along, but she couldn't get her foot back properly into the damp welly. She hobbled along with the welly half on, half off, skidded on the muddy grass and fell into another big puddle.

"What a messy fairy," sniffed Miss Snippersnap's girls. "Don't come anywhere near us."

"She just slipped, that's all," said Buttercup and Tingle.

"It could happen to anyone in this weather," said Cherri and Honeysuckle.

"It wouldn't happen to me," smirked Scary Fairy.

But the rest of Fairy Gropplethorpe's fairies just glared at her and gathered round Airy Fairy and helped her up.

"Now here is a list of three things you have to hunt for," said Miss Stickler. "The first fairy to return with all three items will win a large bag of luscious lollipops."

"Oh, is that all," sniffed Miss Snippersnap's fairies. "We thought it would at least be a box of super de luxe chocolates."

"I'm sure to win the prize anyway," said Scary Fairy, "since I'm the cleverest fairy." And she set off immediately with her list.

Airy Fairy looked at hers. She had to find a four-leaved clover, a seed from a dandelion clock and a petal from a buttercup.

"Come on, everyone," said Twink and Plink. "Scary Fairy's got a head start. Let's catch her up."

All the fairies found a buttercup petal right away. The field was full of buttercups. Airy

Fairy rolled hers up and put it into the pocket of her anorak. Then she started looking for a dandelion seed.

"Oh, we've found ours already. This is too easy." Miss Snippersnap's fairies gave a sniff. Big mistake. They sniffed their dandelion seeds right up their snooty noses.

"Ooh," they cried. "How horrid." And they got out their dainty handkerchiefs and began to blow and blow.

Airy Fairy grinned, found her dandelion seed, and tucked it carefully into the pocket of her anorak.

"Just the four-leaved clover to find now," she said. "Miss Stickler will be pleased if one of our fairies wins the prize."

But it was very hard to find a four-leaved clover, especially in the rain. All the fairies were still searching, including Scary Fairy.

"I want that prize. I must be the one to find it," she muttered.

But she wasn't.

Airy Fairy stopped in her search to empty out her welly again, and there on the grass, right where she was hopping about on one foot, was a four-leaved clover.

"I found it. I found it," she yelled, slipping and sliding on the wet grass as she held it up above her head. "I found a four-leaved clover."

"Oh no you haven't," muttered Scary Fairy, and took out her wand to whisk it away.

But Fairy Gropplethorpe's other fairies had been keeping an eye on Scary Fairy.

"Oh no you don't," they said, and whisked Scary Fairy's wand away from her and dropped it in the stream.

Scary Fairy had no choice but to wade in after it. "Ooh, aah, a-a-atishoo. I'll get you for this," she sneezed, as she flapped about in the muddy water.

But the fairies paid her no heed. They just hurried back with Airy Fairy to collect the prize.

Miss Stickler was pleased that one of her fairies had won. "I just didn't think it would be you, Airy Fairy," she said. "Well done."

"We didn't want the silly lollipops anyway," sniffed Miss Snippersnap's fairies and stomped delicately off.

"Fine," grinned Airy Fairy. "That means more for us," and she shared the lollipops out among her friends.

"I don't want one ob dem eider," muttered Scary Fairy, as she slunk back into her tent to change into dry clothes.

The fairies looked at each other and giggled. They were just enjoying their lollipops when there was an unexpected arrival.

"Look," cried Airy Fairy, pointing to the sky. "It's Elvis Elf's Fairy Tour bus."

Everyone watched as the Fairy Tour bus

zoomed down from the sky, juddered through the muddy field and came to a halt beside the fairies.

Out hopped Rainbow and MacDuff followed by Fairy Gropplethorpe.

"Good news, fairies," she beamed. "The school roof wasn't as bad as I thought and now I can start my summer holiday too. But I've just seen the weather forecast. It's going to stay very wet around here, but it's nice and sunny at the seaside. So I've come to take you all there instead."

"Hurrah," cried all the fairies, except Scary Fairy. She could only croak.

Miss Stickler shook her head. "I'm afraid this wet weather has been bad for poor Scary Fairy. She can't possibly come with you. I'll take her back to school, and put her to bed instead."

"Oh, what a shame," said the other fairies, and tried not to laugh.

The fairies climbed on to the bus and Elvis Elf helped Airy Fairy put her rucksack into the boot. He made sure she was safe inside the bus this time.

Then Fairy Gropplethorpe said, "Right Mr Elf. Take Miss Stickler and Scary Fairy back to school then take the rest of us to the seaside."

"Right away, Fairy Gropplethorpe," grinned Elvis Elf and switched on his engine.

Airy Fairy sat back in her seat and smiled happily. "I knew I was right to pack my bucket and spade," she said to Tingle and Buttercup. "I just love the seaside."

Meet Airy Fairy.
Her wand is all wonky, her wings
are covered in sticking plaster
and her spells are always a muddle!
But she's the cutest fairy around!

Look out for the other books
in this series...

Margaret Ryan

Airy Fairy

Magic Muddle!

How can one little
fairy get into such
BIG trouble?

SCHOLASTIC

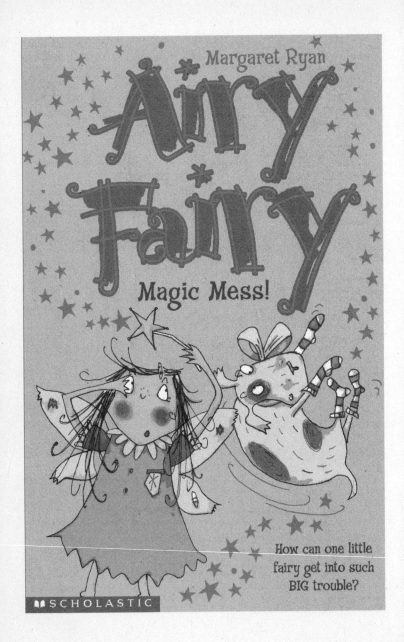

Margaret Ryan

Airy Fairy

Magic Mess!

How can one little
fairy get into such
BIG trouble?

SCHOLASTIC

Margaret ██████

Any
Fairy
Magic Mischief!

How can one little
fairy get into such
BIG trouble?

BLOCK LOAN